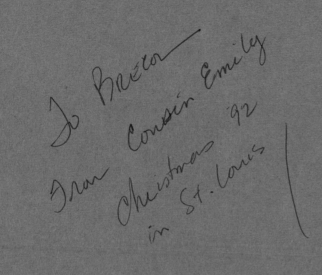

To Brecon
from Cousin Emily
Christmas '92
in St. Louis

ELFWYN'S SAGA

To my teacher,
Charles M. Carr

PHOTOGRAPHY OF CUT-PAPER ILLUSTRATIONS BY LEE SALSBERY

First Edition   1 2 3 4 5 6 7 8 9 10

Library of Congress Cataloging in Publication Data
Wisniewski, David. Elfwyn's saga / by David Wisniewski.   p.   cm. Summary: Although born
blind because of a curse cast on her family by an evil enemy, Elfwyn finds a way to erase the curse
with the help of the Hidden Folk. ISBN 0-688-09589-5.—ISBN 0-688-09590-9 (lib. bdg.) [1. Fairy
tales. 2. Vikings—Fiction.] I. Title.
PZ8.W754E1 1990 [Fic]—dc20   89-35308 CIP AC

ELFWYN'S SAGA

STORY AND PICTURES BY DAVID WISNIEWSKI

LOTHROP, LEE & SHEPARD BOOKS   NEW YORK

It is said that the Hidden Folk dwell unseen in the fire and frost of the North. Glimpsed only in dreams, they bring good to the worthy and ill to the unjust.

Seeing Anlaf Haraldsson and his weary kin searching for land and safe harbor, they directed the waves to carry them gently ashore. But as Gorm the Grim and his warriors raced toward the same spot, the Hidden Folk held back the wind and becalmed their ship.

Gorm bit through his shield in fury, for this meant that Anlaf had won the greenest valley in the North for his own. That night, he carved hateful runes deep in a boulder overlooking the valley, cursing Anlaf and all his line.

Because of the curse, the bright and beautiful daughter of Anlaf and his wife, Gudrun, was born blind.

"This is an ill omen," muttered the midwives. "Such a one should not be permitted to live. Better to let the snow be its blanket."

But Anlaf held the child upon his knee and sprinkled her with water. "You will be called Elfwyn," he proclaimed. "Elfwyn, you are now a member of this house. Sighted or not, be worthy of it."

Horrified that an innocent baby should be blinded by Gorm's cruel curse, the Hidden Folk vowed to teach her to live safely in the valley and help her in time of need.

As a baby, Elfwyn delighted her parents with her happy chatter. As a toddler, she amazed them by never falling down. And as she grew, she astounded all with an endless knowledge of the world around her. "She is beloved of the Hidden Folk," the servants whispered.

On Elfwyn's tenth birthday, Anlaf gave her a sturdy pony and leave to travel the length and breadth of the valley. Gudrun feared for her daughter's safety, especially on the day she saw Elfwyn ride full speed toward a stout limb hanging over her path. But Elfwyn leaned down in her saddle, passed underneath it, and rode on.

"How can you let your child go galloping blind through field and forest?" people would chide Gudrun.

"She is sighted in other ways," Gudrun would calmly reply. "Others should be so blessed."

That Midsummer's Eve, Gorm the Grim strode uninvited into the great hall. A score of his men followed, staggering under the weight of an object wrapped in sail.

"Anlaf Haraldsson," said Gorm, "I bring you this to make amends for the harsh feelings of the past." He drew his sword and cut away the sail. Inside was a huge crystal, clear and perfect, shining with a light of its own. All pressed forward to admire it, all except Elfwyn.

Anlaf and Gudrun bade her join them. She dutifully came forward and placed her hand upon the dazzling surface. "It is hard and cold," she said, "like the man who brought it."

Embarrassed by her curt remark, Anlaf dismissed Elfwyn and thanked Gorm properly for his splendid gift. Gorm bowed silently and left the hall.

As Gudrun gazed into the crystal, she saw herself reflected in its depths—not her present self, but once again a beautiful bride, young and carefree. Anlaf saw himself wielding a king's scepter, ruling lands without limit. Each member of the household received a vision of a wish unearned or a dream unattainable.

Entranced, they remained beside the crystal until dawn. Then they retired to their chambers, tired and newly dissatisfied.

Thus it was that Gorm the Grim sowed seeds of discontent within the clan of Anlaf Haraldsson. Every evening Anlaf and his kin were drawn to the crystal. Within a month, it had drawn out the worst in them. They fell to squabbling and bickering. The valley they had striven for so diligently went untended and unguarded.

Only Elfwyn, protected by her blindness, remained unchanged. She heard the lowing of unmilked cows. She smelled the winter's hay rotting in the fields and felt the rust forming on the idle plows. She ran to tell her father of these things.

"I have no time for that," he said roughly. "I have no time for you." With that, he turned and entered the great hall.

Elfwyn rode into the abandoned fields and wept.

The next morning, as the household slept, Elfwyn led her pony into the great hall. She paced off her distance from the crystal and cast a sturdy noose toward it. Her third attempt was true, and she secured the rope to the pommel of her saddle.

"That is mine, as is everything else," said Gorm. He stepped from the shadows with his men. "You would do well to leave it alone."

Elfwyn urged her pony forward. The rope sprang taut, catching Gorm under the chin. The crystal tilted, then fell with an earsplitting crash, shattering into thousands of pieces. As Elfwyn galloped from the hall, Gorm howled in pain and anger, blinded by the flying fragments.

Awakened by the din, Anlaf Haraldsson and his clan quickly subdued Gorm and his followers. Yet the power of the crystal was not ended. Continuing their flight, the glittering splinters pursued Elfwyn.

At the end of the valley, Elfwyn's exhausted pony stumbled and fell. Elfwyn ran on into unknown land until a huge boulder blocked her way, the one Gorm had carved his curse upon. Turning, she heard the crystal slivers whistling toward her.

The Hidden Folk flew to Elfwyn's aid. At the last moment, they caught hold of her and soared upward. The crystal fragments crashed into the boulder, erasing the curse and destroying themselves.

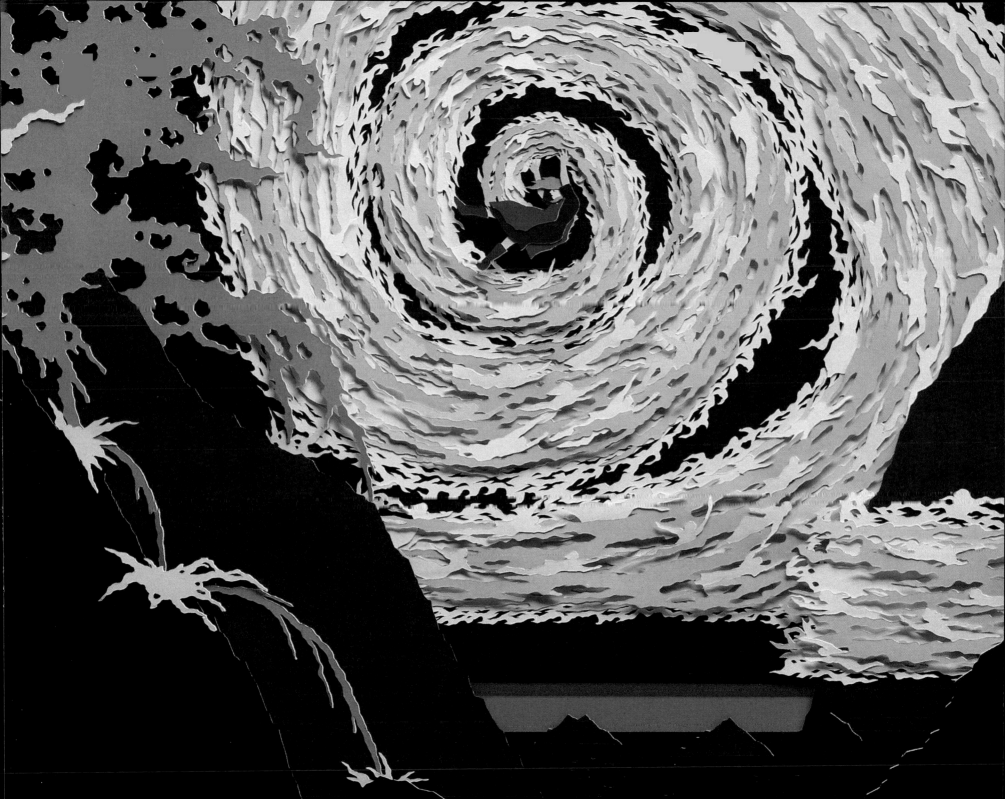

And in that instant, Elfwyn saw. Overjoyed, the Hidden Folk
bore her gently home.

Anlaf Haraldsson and his clan saw, too—saw how their inattention to duty had brought them close to ruin.

Banished forever from the Northlands, Gorm soon perished.

And that is how a household was saved by a girl who, though once blind, had never lost her vision. She became known as Elfwyn the Second-Sighted, and many came to her for counsel.

When you meet the Hidden Folk in a dream, they will tell you this tale is true. To prove it, they will point to the glimmer in the cold, clear skies above that part of the world. We call it the Northern Lights, but it is the dust of the crystal, drifting harmlessly among the stars.

AUTHOR'S NOTE

Attentiveness to duty is always advisable. At times, though, it can become a life-and-death matter. In tenth-century Iceland, in the Viking age, distraction from duty could bring disastrous consequences.

Floki Valgerdarson, one of the first Vikings to visit the island, found this out. He and his kin settled in a green valley near a fjord teeming with fish and seals. Satisfied with hunting, they neglected to make winter hay for their livestock. Bitter cold set in and the animals perished. The settlers were trapped there for a whole year before the pack ice melted and they could escape. Floki named the place Iceland and never returned.

But other Vikings were to follow. (Viking, which means "the act of raiding overseas," became a convenient label for all the fierce bands of Norwegians, Swedes, and Danes who forsook their meager farms for the promise of richer lands across the ocean.)

Gorm the Grim represents the conventional notion of a Viking: a terrifying marauder armed with sword and battle-ax, sailing a fearsome dragon ship and striking without warning. Indeed, Gorm is more formidable than most, belonging to a class of warriors known as berserks, or "bear-shirts," because of the animal skins they often wore. Howling, leaping, and biting their shields, berserks were much prized in battle for their titanic rage and superhuman strength.

Other Vikings, like Anlaf and Gudrun, sailed for new homes and farms rather than adventure and plunder. They advanced the culture of their new homelands, leaving a continuing legacy of government, poetry, and art. In Iceland the settlers formed a republic and instituted the world's first parliament, the Althing. They also kept extensive records. These histories, filled with feuds, love stories, and legends, are known as sagas. Saga means "something said," and the sagas were passed by word of mouth for generations before being committed to paper.

The saga of Elfwyn (a Celtic name meaning "beloved of elves") is original, but draws from Icelandic history and legend.

The Hidden Folk or huldufolk are said to be the descendants of the unwashed children of Eve. When the Lord called, she showed Him the ones she had managed to bathe and pretended to have no others. This angered the Lord greatly. "That which is hidden from me shall forever be hidden from men," He declared. From that time on, they could be glimpsed only in dreams.

Runes were the written alphabet of Scandinavia, similar to those used throughout Europe from the third to the thirteenth century. Runes were regarded as powerful and mysterious. They were used in magic and curses and were carved in stone to commemorate heroes, heroines, and loved ones. Many runestones remain in Scandinavia, but they are very rare in Iceland.

Because food was scarce in the new settlements, deformed or handicapped infants were exposed to the elements to die. Once adopted through the rite of naming and blessing with water, however, a child was a permanent member of the family.

Gorm's mesmerizing crystal is loosely based on the legendary "sunstone." When held toward the sun on an overcast day, this magical gem was reported to glow, making navigation possible.

The Northern Lights (or aurora borealis) are a magnificent display of shimmering light caused by electrically charged particles borne by solar winds colliding with the earth's atmosphere. Their glimmer beautifies the long winter nights in the north.

In preparing the illustrations for this book, I used artistic license upon occasion. Gorm's distinctive helmet is much more decorative than those usually worn, being of earlier Swedish origin. Most Viking warriors (when they had helmets at all) wore the Norman variety, a pointed steel cap with nosebar. Also, though essentially treeless now, the Iceland of Viking times had an abundance of birch trees, considerably slighter than the massive oak beneath which Elfwyn rides her pony.

The illustrations are cut same size from ChromaRama colored papers and adhered with double-stick photo mountings. They are first sketched on layout paper, with a final drawing made on tracing paper. The drawing is then transferred to the back of the colored papers and cut out. An X-Acto knife and over one thousand very sharp blades were used to produce the illustrations for this book. And because I paid attention, I didn't cut myself once.